Jet Is Naughty

Story by Annette Smith

Illustrations by Richard Hoit

Harry said to Mom,

"Can we go down to the park?"

"Not today," said Mom.
"Look at your bedroom."

"Oh," said Harry.

"Jet," said Harry.

"Look at my bedroom.

Will you help me?"

Click! Click! Click!

"Good," said Harry.

"My shoes and my school bag
go in here," said Harry.
"My hat goes in here, too."

Jet looked at Harry's hat.

Click! Click! Click!

"Jet!" cried Harry.

"Come back with my hat.

It goes in here

with my school bag.

You are naughty!"

Click! Click! Click!

Jet came down
with Harry's hat.

"Stay down here, Jet,"
said Harry.
"You are not a helicopter."

"Jet!" said Harry.

"Here comes Mom.

Get into your box."

Click! Click! Click!

Jet went inside his box.

"Your bedroom looks good,"
said Mom.

"We **will** go down to the park."